SARAH LLEWELLYN

Engulfed

AUSTIN MACAULEY PUBLISHERS™
LONDON • CAMBRIDGE • NEW YORK • SHARJAH

A CIP catalogue record for this title is available from the British
Library.

ISBN 9781398459625 (Paperback)
ISBN 9781398459632 (ePub e-book)

www.austinmacauley.com

First Published 2022
Austin Macauley Publishers Ltd
1 Canada Square
Canary Wharf
London E14 5AA

ABOUT THE AUTHOR

Sarah is and always has been an avid reader, with the imagination to go with it. Each story she pored over inspired her to one day achieve that quiet but constant dream within her: to see her name written at the bottom of a book. Living a simple life with a big dream, Sarah used the 2020/21 lockdown to pursue this, and so this is her debut to the world.

DEDICATION

To my Mum and Dad, for never letting me go a day without letting
me know how much you love me.

To my Alex, for giving me your love and support with no shadow of a
doubt. There are no chapters, so no excuses.

ACKNOWLEDGEMENTS

Firstly, I would like to thank my parents. They encouraged my love of reading from the earliest age; my fondest memories of Christmas would be organising the piles of books that they had bought me. They have supported me every day in order to make my world a happier place, and through everything, they are my best friends.

A world of gratitude needs to go to my Alex who has listened to my every worry and tried to solve every problem for me just to bring the smile to my face once more.

Thank you to my family, who were so excited by this that they wanted to be the ones to play the characters in a movie one day.

Lastly, thank you to Austin Macauley, for taking a leap of faith with me: you have made my dream come true and for that, I am eternally grateful.

IT CAME SUDDENLY. Not slow and drawn out like we had thought. Abruptly. Life as we knew would never be the same again. Life as we knew, just wouldn't be. There was no fighting it. No beating it. There were no superheroes coming to save the day. When you watch a film, this is the moment where it seems like all is lost, all is over and the bad has won and the good is dying out. In the movie, though, there is this unexpected last triumph where the good defies all odds. Defies the norm. Defies rational explanation and suddenly, somehow, they have won. You don't question the plausibility of it or the way it happened. You accept it. You accept that good always wins.

Except that, that is the movie version. The novel version. Not the real-life version. And in reality, we appear to have run out of the magic that helps us defy all odds. They tried to warn us years ago. Stop global warning, recycle, reduce your carbon footprint. They tried to prepare us and give us the opportunity to change our destiny but we were too selfish to listen. It wasn't harming us there and then, so why the hell should we care? We live in a day and age where everything is so easily accessible to our front door with no input from ourselves besides the easy click of a button, so easy in fact that you forget about the huge and draining process it took to get it to your doorstep within hours of ordering it. We simply took advantage of it and didn't look back. That was our new norm. We had progressed so much in so few years that it felt as though hover cars and robots were a soon to be plausible addition to our world.

Except, this is our lot now and we have to accept it. All we have done in life has amounted to nothing, all the great and wonderful things that happened in history before the world became so selfish have come to mean absolutely nothing.

My story isn't the beginning or the middle. It is the end of the end. It was over before it could ever really begin. A tale of nothing and everything.

The world stopped in a heartbeat. We were given a mere forty-eight hours. If that. It seemed cruel. Suddenly next-day delivery meant nothing, but getting ourselves to our family the next day meant everything. Those who weren't within driving distance of their family didn't have a hope in hell of returning to them to be with them. Those who did manage to get to them would feel as though the time spent with them just wasn't long enough. Nothing was enough now.

* * *

"The heat from the sun will engulf the earth within the next forty-eight hours." The man on the television before us looks bedraggled, like he hasn't had a wash or a good night's sleep in quite a while and I wonder just how long he has known about this. I ponder to myself, asking myself an array of what ifs. What if he had told us sooner, would we have been able to do anything about it? What if we had had more time with family? What if we had been able to make a difference?

Luke and I sit watching the screen, listening to what they were saying. The words feel too loud and harsh. The broadcast is on repeat on every channel and has been for a few hours now but this is the first time we have fully watched it. Both having rushed home after being let go from our jobs, we scrambled through the door together, our little whippet, Cassie, racing up to meet us, confused by why her owners had brushed past her, barely acknowledging each other let alone her as we turned the television on, neither of us quite believing what everyone had been telling us. None of it felt real.

Luke sits on the edge of his seat and I kneel on the floor in front of the television anxiously listening. Cassie has wormed her way between my legs, our precious little girl wondering what on earth is going on as she begs to be petted, whining and pawing at my arm. I stroke her absent-mindedly as I listen to the television and this instantly halts her whines, but I feel the tension in her body.

"There is no way to survive this. This is the end of the world. Spend your time wisely with family and loved ones. Say your goodbyes and pray. Pray that there is another life beyond this one. A better life. A life where we unconsciously learn from our mistakes."

The man chokes up as he walks off screen, ripping out his microphone, jerking at his tie and pulling out a black flask from his dishevelled and creased suit jacket and gulping back what I can only imagine is a very strong drink. The sight it is somehow sobering. History in the making. The camera flashes back to a news broadcast lady and she looks solemn and broken but in control. Her hair is immaculate and her suit creaseless. She and her co-star have been handed the unpleasant task of telling the world our time has come to an end. No greater burden has ever existed.

"So, there you have it, this is the last broadcast being announced. This will replay until the end to make people aware, but the world will now slowly grind to a halt as we return to our families and spend the little time we have left simply being with them."

Tears drip down her cheeks, mascara running as silent tears start to rip through her body and it is one of the most heart-breaking sights. "Goodnight and goodbye," she whispers, fluffing her papers in front of her, sniffing loudly.

"Luke."

I whisper his name as he switches off the television, but not before the President's face lights up the television. He looks no different to ever. Calm and in control. Maybe that's good. Maybe that's bad. I just don't know. Maybe now is the time to see such an elusive figure show emotion. Either way, Luke turns the television off. Hearing it once is enough. We don't need to hear it again from someone else's mouth.

"Maya." He mirrors my reaction, his voice a shadow of despair and hopelessness.

Neither of us knows what to say. How to make this better.

"We'll go to your family," he whispers after several beats of silence and I look at him, shocked by his omission.

"What about yours?" I query, knowing his strained relationship with his parents. His mother is deep in the late stages of dementia and his father has devoted his life to looking after her and keeping her out of a home as long as he possibly can. Nothing else matters to him, not even his own son anymore. The only good thing I can see out of all this is that they will die alongside one another. At peace together. Not one left without the other.

"We will go see them first as soon as we can and then we will head up to your parents; it's eight hours away, so we need to get on the road soon. Everything will be gridlocked with people doing the same thing, just trying to get to their families," he explains and stands up, looking around, trying to form a plan in his mind.

"Luke." I whisper once more, looking up at my husband, my brand new and shiny husband, our wedding bands not yet tarnished by life. Two months into our marriage and still awaiting our honeymoon. We hadn't had time to embrace our life together yet. I can't help but wonder when I'll wake up from this nightmare. When will someone jump out from behind the curtains and tell us it's a prank and we have won an obscene amount of money?

"Maya." His voice breaks and I stand up, moving into his arms, Cassie wanders around our feet before retreating to her little bed and I know in an instant she is sulking. I feel sick. This can't be real. This can't be happening.

"We won't have a life together," I whisper and he tries to shush me, stroking my back softly. "No Luke, we can't ignore this, we are going to die soon and we won't have had a life together." I claw at my chest, anxiety pouring down my throat like acid, churning my stomach. I think I'm going to be sick.

"What good will come of talking about it?" He snaps at me and tears form in my eyes. He doesn't snap. He doesn't get angry. Luke is the epitome of calm. Something I have always loved about him. In this moment, though, I see a scared and fearful young man who, for the first time in his life, doesn't know how to make this better. Someone who doesn't have an answer for me. Google won't help us now.

"Because I want to imagine it all. Imagine how wonderful it would have been." I gasp for air as the tears come thick and fast. "We wouldn't have been in this hovel that we call home much longer. We would have moved into our glorious house for life after all the skimping and saving we have done. We have worked so hard for so long to such a detriment. It hardly seems worth it now. We forgot to live whilst planning to live."

I am furious at us for not going on expensive holidays like our honeymoon or eating at mouth-watering restaurants. I am furious we never started to create a bucket list, let alone got the chance to complete it.

"How many more pets?" he whispers and I look up at him and the look of calm has returned to his eyes as he joins me on this imaginary path. I close my eyes letting myself be enveloped by the possibility of our future.

"Countless. Cats, dogs, hamsters for the kids, rabbits and fish, chickens, and birds."

He chuckles at my list and, even with my eyes closed, I know he is rolling his own and it makes me smile.

"So basically, you want to buy a zoo," he murmurs teasingly and I'm glad he can still smile and make me smile at a time such as this. "Cassie will be jealous. Look at her, she's sulking now!" He gestures to her before returning his arm around me quickly, as if scared to let go for too long.

"She'll get over it! Our kids need to grow up knowing how to care for things." I smile softly, opening my eyes to look at our little rescue dog. She has been spoilt rotten since we got there. A right diva.

"Our kids, yeah?" He smiles at the thought, pulling me even closer to him, as if that is possible, as I lay my head on his chest. We stand in the middle of our small living room, the walls a deep green, making the room feel smaller than it really is. The paint cans were sitting in the corner ready to transform it into a serene white. They had been sat there so long, I'm not even sure the paint can be used anymore.

"Yeah, three. The third one would have been an accident no doubt but a beautiful one at that. A girl and two boys. A girl should always know what it is like to grow up with brothers who will torment and bully her but will always protect her like the princess she is," I whisper, my thoughts turning to my own two older brothers. Dexter and Peter. They riled me up and picked on me endlessly as we grew up but they were there. There were *always* there. Every little girl should have a big brother. Or two.

"Got any names for our children?" He whispers and I feel his hot salty tears splashing down onto my cheeks, only breaking my heart further.

"No, I was waiting to see what they looked like when they were born," I sob into his chest, feeling grief for the children we will never have. Feeling as though they have died before they have lived and wondering if this feeling is even close to the grief of a parent losing a child.

My phone starts to ring and I reluctantly pull away from Luke. He grabs my hand before I can turn away from him and looks me in the eyes. His chocolate brown eyes. The ones I haven't grown tired of gazing into yet.

"It was a wonderful life and I have loved every minute of it with you." He leans down to kiss my forehead, lingering a beat too long, but not long enough, and walks away before we both dissolve into more tears. If only time could stand still. I grab my ringing phone off the side and I answer it, spotting my mother's face on the caller ID.

"Hey, Mom." My voice sounds hoarse and the words feel like tar in my mouth.

"Maya, what's going on? I don't understand." Her voice is thick with confusion and tears and I can hear banging around in the background. "Your father is saying that the world is ending but I feel like he is being dramatic."

"No, Mom, he isn't being dramatic, you need to listen to him, the world is ending. We don't have long," I whisper and the silence from her tells me she finally believes it. "I'm sorry."

"Come home," she begs. "Please come home."

"I'm trying. We need to go see Luke's parents first but then we will come straight home to you, I promise." I explain to her our plan but she doesn't want to hear it.

"No! No, please, just come straight home to us, we don't want to lose out on time with you," she demands; the only acceptable type of selfish, from a mom needing her child by her side.

"No, Mom." *I'm sorry.* "Luke needs me just as much as you do. We will get to you in time, I promise."

I plead with her but I know how much she hates being this far away from me as it is. She protested so much to Luke and I moving across the country but she knew we were doing it for a better future, to be able to provide something more for our children.

"Please," she begs. I can hear Dad scrambling around in the background calling her name.

"We will be home soon. Are Dexter and Peter at yours?" I ask, trying to distract her.

"Not yet, they were supposed to be coming over today for dinner anyway, I am going to call them now." She sounds placated for now and I decide to let her go.

15

"Go call them, Mom." I sigh softly, worrying we won't be in time and this will be the last time I hear her voice. "Mommy?" I gulp at my worry.

"Yes, dear?" She listens closely, like the perfect mom she has always been.

"This isn't goodbye," I announce.

"It feels like it, baby." She breathes down the phone heavily and I can feel my mother's heart breaking. A mother needs to protect her children and all she can do is wait. It must be agonising for her.

"No, we will make it in time, I promise." I grit my teeth, determined. "I love you and I will see you soon."

I put the phone down before she can say anything. I look at the texts I have received and both my brothers are checking in on me and making sure I am on my way home. I return the text and confirm my well-being and my ETA.

I will make it.

I have to make it.

* * *

"Get some more clothes if you want them and anything else now, Maya, but nothing that is not essential. We need to leave now," Luke demands as he walks back into the room, holding a small holdall full for him and handing a second empty one to me.

I take it and run through the house and it suddenly feels like I am in one of my nightmares where I have to pack my bag to go on holiday whilst my lift to the airport is at my door already. I am running out of time and I can't think what is essential and what isn't. I grab some spare clothes and I look around the room in despair. What do I take with me? What really matters? I rub my face, looking down at my outfit from work and I quickly strip, changing everything, pulling on comfy leggings and a long top. I tug on my trainers. I twist at my wedding and engagement rings out of habit and I suddenly run to the bookshelves, pulling out loads of different albums trying to find my and Luke's album. Our wedding album. I hold it close to my chest before I shove it into the bag. I don't know why but there is a part of me that tells me I need it. I go to the toilet quick before walking back out to Luke who is on the phone to his parents.

"I am coming, I promise. I am on my way," he whimpers down the phone and I can hear his father shouting and I spot the tears staining Luke's face and I hate it. I want to take him away from all this. I want to keep him safe. "I can't stay, you know I can't, I have to get Maya to her parents."

My heart breaks as I realise that Luke won't be with his parents when the time comes. Maybe they can come with us.

"No, Maya, stay out of this, they can't," Luke waves me away and I realise I have said it out loud. "Bye dad, we will see you soon," and he snaps the phone down and I despise the feeling in the room. The anger and the upset and something else. It is bitter and it leaves a bad taste in my mouth.

Resentment.

"Luke, you can bring your parents to mine," I allow him, treading carefully this time but he shakes his head at my suggestion.

"I tried. I really tried. Dad wants Mum somewhere she knows." He tears his hands through his hair and growls before letting out an emotionless chuckle. "God knows why, she remembers fuck all."

I walk over to my ball of anger; he stares out the window, desolate and an island. I have never seen him like this. Then again, I suppose I have never seen the world like this. I can't expect his normal behaviour when this isn't a normal situation.

"You don't mean that," I whisper, taking his hand.

"No, I know, I just, I can't bear this."

He stutters over his words, frustration getting to him, and he pulls his hand out of mine. He looks down at me with cold expectant eyes and I feel a shiver go through me. He sighs for what feels like the millionth time before pulling me to his side, trying to take the sting out of ripping his hand away from me.

"No, I suspect no one can, but all we can do now is make the most of this minute amount of time and accept that it is all we have." I assert myself, trying to calm his worries.

"Since when did you turn into a little philosopher?" Luke queries, raising his eyebrow, incredibly bemused.

"Since I found out I only have forty-eight hours to live," I chuckle and suddenly the laughs come deeper and hard. Luke joins me and we laugh together until our tummies hurt and until tears fall from our eyes that aren't related to sadness. When we finally come to, silence echoes through the room abruptly and it's like nothing ever happened as we return to our solemn and quiet selves.

"Get Cassie ready and let's go." He takes my holdall from me and walks out the front door.

I walk over to Cassie, having packed some food and her favourite little cuddly toy, a miniature version of herself. I clip her leash on and she glares up at me, still sulking from having been ignored.

"We have to go now Cassie, time to go see Nanny and Grandad."

I smile softly at her and stroke her behind the ears exactly where she loves it and she instantly melts against my hand and begs for more from me. I take the moment to savour our little dog. Smaller than most Whippets, she was definitely the runt of the litter. Having been left on the side of the road and starved, she still carried a small form with a large appetite for life and food. Mainly food. The feeling was mutual when we laid eyes on her in the dog rescue centre that fateful day and the rest was history. She was the perfect dog. Quiet, sweet-tempered and loyal. She made our little house a home.

I take her leash and grab the keys, although for what reason I don't know: it's not like we will ever need to get back in. I take one more look at our tiny little house. Barely big enough for us. We have moaned about it for so long, hating so much about it. So ready to move on and find a bigger and better home once we had the deposit saved up. But now, as I look at it, I can't see anything bad. I see the front door where Luke carried me over the threshold on our wedding night. I see the stains on the carpet beneath the sofa where we sit and eat our dinners each night because we don't have room for a dining table. I see the dent in the wall where I threw a book at Luke once when we were having a fight. I see the love and the warmth and the fact that it is our home. I don't want to say goodbye.

Goodbye.

I lock the door behind me, pocketing my keys and walking out to the car, climbing in the passenger seat, letting Cassie hop up and into the back seat before I strap myself in and ready myself for the journey. I look at my watch and see it has been an hour already.

"Forty-seven hours," I state.

"We don't know that we will get that much time. It might be sooner: the broadcast has been going for a few hours, which is why we have to get going."

Luke starts the engine and we drive off down the street. I look at my neighbours' homes and everything feels so eerie and quiet. Like the world has gone to ground. I suppose it has. I send them a silent prayer, hoping their last moments are happy.

* * *

We pull up outside Luke's parents' house. A small but quaint little cottage. We visit every week but it feels like I am seeing it for the first time ever right now. I stare at the pale green colour of the exterior, the peeling white windows and the cracks shattering the walls.

It needs a lot of tender loving care but that hasn't been high up on Eric's list since Rose, his wife, was diagnosed with dementia. Luke found it harder than I expected. He didn't know how to respond when his mother had no idea who he was and as an only child he had no one to turn to for help. His father was too consumed with making life as normal as possible for Rose. It was a distressing story of love. Luke waves to me to get out of the car and I do, breaking out of my stupor, annoyed at myself for wasting time looking at a house that will soon be ashes. It is what is inside that matters. Or rather who is inside. Looking back on Cassie, she is sound asleep snuggled up with her comfort and so I leave the windows open for her and return to Luke's side. Where I belong.

"Hello, son." Eric opens the door and shakes his son's hand so formally and I can see the relationship is as strained as ever. Eric looks past Luke to me and lets out a grunt. They used to be such a perfect little family, so content with having each other, but when Rose was diagnosed, everything around them crumbled.

"Hm, brought the wife, I see," he snipes, and I ignore it.

Eric grew resentful and bitter towards his son after Rose was diagnosed. He berated him for not coming around more often but when Luke tried, he was met with criticism and a cold front. I endlessly defended my husband and Eric forgot how much we got on when they were all happy. Now he simply tolerated me because of Luke and because of how good I was with his wife. I was able to calm and soothe her like no one else could. Not even Eric. He despised it. Luke struggled to know how to act around his mum now. It used to cause him and his mum so much upset at the beginning as he almost argued with her when she told him he was her son, or that her sister was still alive or that she needed to get to work. I taught him to placate her and go along with things to keep her calm and comfortable. Sometimes that is the best way.

"Hi Eric, nice to see you." I smile at him but it feels awkward and forced and I realise I have no idea how to act. We are going to die soon. How am I meant to act in this scenario?

"Nice to see me?" he scoffs. "Never liked each other, have we, but you're always so polite," he grumbles. "Can't fault you there."

He walks away from me and I hold back my anger. We once laughed and laughed together. He can't have forgotten everything from before, can he? His whole world revolves around Rose these days. I shouldn't expect anything more. I want to hand it to him, finally tell him what I think about him but I can't, this isn't the time or the place and it wouldn't be fair on Luke to cause such an argument when we have so little time. There is also the sane, empathetic part of me that knows deep down I would do the same for Luke if the tables were turned. How awful it must be to have your world slip away to a stranger.

"Please don't be rude to Maya," Luke snaps at his father and stalks past him towards his mum's room.

"Don't go in there, she is sleeping. I'll tell her your goodbyes," Eric hisses, rushing past him to try and block his son's path.

"I don't give a fuck if she is sleeping, I am going to see her and say goodbye, she is my mother." Luke pushes past his father and through the door, his eyes ablaze and I see my husband in a light that I have never seen before. Desperate.

"Not like it matters anyway, we'll all be dead soon and she won't remember you." Eric's voice wavers. "Or me."

"Eric!" I gasp at his harsh words and he looks at me and I see a broken man. A man who has nothing left and whose wife won't know what is happening when it comes to the end; a blessing, and a curse.

"What?" he responds dejectedly as he slumps himself into one of the two armchairs placed next to each other.

"I'm sorry." I move over to him, sitting in the vacant armchair and take his hand. Despite our differences, I can't bear seeing him like this.

"What are you sorry about? Me being a bastard to you and Luke?" He sighs heavily, like the weight of the world is on his shoulders. "No, it's me that needs to be sorry. I haven't made it easy for you or him. It's just so hard being here with her all the time, never being remembered but remembering everything." He squeezes my hand tightly. "Look after him," he demands and I nod fervently.

"Without a doubt. I love him, Eric, always have done, always will." I smile softly at him.

"I know, you look at him the way his mother used to look at me." He chuckles. "The way only a fool in love does. It will only ever break your heart."

"I wouldn't say a fool; it's one of the best feelings in the world, loving someone." I contemplate a life where Luke hadn't been a part of it and I know how bland and boring it would have been. As humans, we crave and need relations with other humans. It is vital to our emotional well-being. Life without it just isn't quite life at all.

"I suppose you're right." He releases my hand and stands up. "Let's go say goodbye."

"I'll give you all some time. I'll say goodbye to Rose when you are finished as a family."

I shrug softly, not wanting to intervene on this moment. It is a once in a lifetime moment and not a welcome one but it is all we have now and I won't come between Luke and his father. They need to reconcile before it is too late. Eric nods and walks into Rose's room, closing the door. I listen to the whispers and murmurings coming from within and I can only hope that it is doing some good. If there is only one good thing that comes from all this awfulness then let it be this. A family brought back together at the last moment.

* * *

I sit staring at nothing for ages. Nothing good comes from spare time when contemplating rapidly approaching death. I think about Luke and how we had planned a life together, I think about how I had hoped that one day soon, within the year or so, I would be pregnant with our first child. We were young still but I wanted to be fresh and sprightly whilst my children were in their early years. We had also planned our adventures for after the children were grown up and had flown the nest. We had accepted a life of hard work to make it possible but we knew what we wanted. *Doesn't matter now.* My cruel thoughts attack me and bring me down. I don't have a future anymore. Not now. No one does.

It feels like they are in the bedroom forever and it feels like a place I don't belong. I belong with my family. With my mum and dad who are so family-oriented and who hated us moving to the city for work. With my brothers who have stayed close to home, both building a business together. I was the youngest yet the first to marry. Dexter and Peter hadn't sown their wild oats yet and weren't ready for commitment. We grew up tattling on each other for the least little thing, they had tickled me until I wet myself because it was funny and bribed me into saying swear words only to tell on me to Mum straight away. Mum knew, though; she always knew what her boys were like. When it had come down to it, though, and I needed help, they were there. They beat Samuel Roberts for me when he kept bullying me for having braces, they shouted at the teacher who shouted at me because I left my homework at home, despite the fact it had been my brothers who had taken it out of my bag. They were my brothers and my best friends. I couldn't wait to see them again. It had been too long as it is. Now it wasn't going to be long enough.

The door finally opens and I exhale a sigh of relief. My anxiety had been getting the better of me and I felt like, any moment, the world would end and I wouldn't be with my family. I would be alone in a room. All by myself.

Luke walks to me and takes my hands in his, leaning in to kiss my temple before leading me to the bedroom to see Rose.

"Time to say goodbye, we need to get going soon," he comments as we walk in. Rose looks beautiful but frail. She smiles when she sees me, just like she always does.

"Hi Rose, it's lovely to see you, you're looking beautiful today, I like the way you've done your hair." I smile softly as I kneel beside the bed, taking her hand in mine and stroking it. I know that Eric will have done her hair this morning along with her 'lippie', as she calls it. She loves her routine and it keeps her rooted.

"You must be Luke's wife, you're very beautiful." She tries to grip my hand but her strength is lacking, so I do it for her.

"Maya." I state my name.

"I know, I remember." She laughs softly. "I'm not silly, you only came last week." I blink in shock. This is the first time she has remembered me in such a long time. "Did you bake that cake you were planning on attempting?"

I nod dumbfounded and Luke falls to his knees beside me, just as shocked as I am. He grabs her hand out of mine, gripping it tightly and bringing it to his lips as he starts to cry.

"Oh Luke, my little baby Luke, I'm so proud of you," she whispers softly, lifting her other hand to stroke his face. He closes his eyes and bathes himself in her touch. It reminds me so much of a young and innocent boy needing his mother's love. He has been starved of it for so long. She forgot he existed a long time ago and lucid moments when we happened to be around were rare.

"Mama."

He chokes on the word and I immediately move out the way so he can be closer to his mum. I feel horrendous that we have to go soon. We need to leave and I don't want to be the one to say it but I can't risk not being with my family. I let him talk with her a bit longer as he tells her all about how he and I met and how he proposed and our wedding. He tells her everything about him. It's like he can't stop talking and like he never wants to. I look at Eric and he is sitting in the chair in the corner watching his wife and son and he looks at peace. He looks at me, catching me watching him and he smiles sadly, nodding gently.

"Son." He clears his throat as he speaks, trying to hide the choke of tears, I suspect. "I think it's time you get your wife to her family."

I cringe inside as Luke looks at me as though he had forgotten I was there, and I can't fault him for doing so: he is spending the first proper time with his mum in years. I thank God that it happened now.

"I'm sorry, Luke," I mutter. "I wish we could stay longer." I blush and hate myself. I hate tearing him away from this.

"It's okay." He comforts me with a lie before turning back to his mum. "We have to get going, Mum, but please, please remember how much I love you." He leans in to hug her close. His whole body shakes as he starts to cry.

"I love you too, Luke. Don't you worry about me, your father takes great care of me." She smiles at her husband over her shoulder before turning her gaze to me. "Look after him for me, Maya, I'm entrusting you with my baby boy."

I nod softly, hating that I've already failed. I can't succeed at the impossible and I can't save him from this. No one can.

Luke moves away so I can say my goodbyes, kissing Rose on the cheek before embracing Eric genuinely for the first time in a long time. I move out of the room and inform Luke I'll be in the car when he is ready and I leave the house. I walk out to the car, getting in the driver's seat, deciding to take the first shift of driving. We have a nearly eight-hour drive ahead of us and I'm not looking forward to a single moment of it. I just want to go home. It's the same feeling you have as you wait on the last day of your holiday for the coach to arrive to take you to the airport. You just want to be home with a click of your fingers.

An ominous feeling flows over me and I can't help but feel

25

uneasy about something. *The world is ending, you moron. Of course you feel uneasy!* My subconscious berates and belittles me for feeling so anxious. It doesn't help in the slightest.

I look at Luke in his home, talking to his dad on the doorstep, his father stoic and solid like usual, but his red eyes tell a different story. I notice the temperature is a lot higher: the intensity of it is increasing, and I realise that we are getting closer to the end and it feels unbearable already. I look at my watch once more and whimper, seeing that we have forty-four hours left. If that. If we left now and had no breaks or sleep then we would arrive with 36 hours to spend with them and I hate that Luke gets three hours and I get potentially thirty-six. Maybe we can stay a bit longer. *I don't want to, though.* The selfish and honest part of me rears its ugly head. As much as I love Luke, his family don't mean as much to me as my own. Luke and my family matter to me more than anything. I think about how it must be the same for him: his family matters more to him than mine, and yet he is sacrificing such a sacred and special time to make me happy. To make me feel safe. To be with me. I sigh softly, biting at my nails. Luke looks at me in the car and waves softly, holding up one finger, telling me he'll only be a moment. A moment is everything. My heart starts to shatter as I contemplate the next few hours. This is going to hurt. My thoughts suddenly turn to how it will feel physically when the end comes. Will it hurt? Will it be quick or long and drawn-out? Will we know it is happening? Question after question plagues my mind, turning it to darkness as my very human fear of death makes a grand entrance.

"Hey." The door opens and Luke gets in the passenger seat. He doesn't put his seat belt on. He sits, staring out the front window. I mirror his behaviour.

"Hey," I whisper and we sit in silence together.

Luke takes my hand and kisses it gently as we sit in silence. I sit motionless for as long as I can because I can't bear what comes

26

next. Before long, I know we cannot sit here any longer without saying anything.

"You aren't coming with me, are you?" I croak, gripping his hand tight. The silence continues and I feel him move beside me, leaning over to pull me out of my seat and over the handbrake and straight into his lap, into his arms, into him.

"I can't, Maya," he whispers into my ear as he buries his face into my hair.

"I know."

I start to sob and I don't feel like I will ever be able to stop. We hold each other because it is the end of the world. We hold each other close because this is a choice we never thought we would have to make. How could we be without each other when we had promised one another forever and longer in our wedding vows? We are each other's safe place, refuge, nirvana. Whatever you want to call it. We belong together.

I cry until I can't cry anymore. I gasp for air because it doesn't feel like it comes naturally anymore. I beg. I beg for the end to come now. I beg that we don't have to make this decision. I beg that it be taken out of our hands before we have to tear ourselves away from each other. We were normal people, who turned into a normal couple, who hoped to have a normal life with a normal family. Except this wasn't normal.

The sobs turn to silence and our breathing returns to normal after what felt like an eternity and as we stay quiet and glued to each other in that passenger seat outside his parents' house, we silently know that this is the only way it could be. We love each other enough to know and to accept that, right now, our families need us more. We are strong enough to know our love is a forever in itself. There is no need to stand hand in hand by each other's side when the sun finally blazes us to ashes. Somehow, despite the heartbreak that would come from turning the engine on and driving away without him next to me, without any words between us,

27

I know it would all be okay. Our love shines brighter than the sun ever could.

"Maya, you have to go now," Luke instructs and when I look up at him, I see his matching red raw eyes and puffy face. He is trying so hard not to cry once more. He is trying to be strong for me.

"I'm sorry," I whisper and he grabs my face to make me look at him.

"I'm not and neither should you be. This is bigger than us. This isn't our decision, but we can't allow our parents to be without their children at the end." His lower lip stiffens as he tries to toughen up. "I love you, till the end of the world and beyond that; nothing can change that, not even the sun engulfing us."

"I love you too. I have loved our life together even if we didn't get to live out our plans," I murmur softly, stroking his face, trying to memorise every last detail of him. The little raised mole above his left eyebrow, the dark bags beneath his molten chocolate eyes and the small chicken pox scar on his left cheek that has turned into a dimple as he has got older. I won't see him go grey. I won't see his laughter lines meet the rest of the wrinkles that will mar his face one day.

"We'll live it out up here." He points to my mind and then to my chest. "And in here." I nod and I agree.

"Goodbye, Luke," I whisper. I feel sick.

"Goodbye, Maya," he returns the comment and we sit once more in silence, simply gazing at each other.

An hour must go past as darkness creeps down on us. Neither of us says another word. We simply exist together a little longer.

"Time for you to go."

He utters the words that I don't want to hear and I nod. I climb over to the driver's side. Looking in the back, I see the provisions that Luke put in the car as food and drink and I reach over to grab his holdall, giving it to him. He hoists out a top of his and hands it to me, knowing how much I love to fall asleep with his shirt on. I smile gratefully and clutch it to my chest and watch him as he lifts Cassie out from the back seat and snuggles her into his arms affectionately. She licks at his face and snuggles him frantically, excited her usually gruff Daddy is paying attention to her. She has always been first and foremost my dog, loyal to a tee, but she is a secret Daddy's girl wannabe.

"Look after her for me, Cassie," he whispers, gazing at her as if trying to memorise her little face, and she lets out a soft whine as if answering him.

He starts to climb out of the car and leaves Cassie in his warmed-up seat which she immediately settles down into. *Don't go!* I bite back the tears as I start the car, stroking Cassie's head softly for reassurance as I watch Luke walk to the door. *Please, don't go.* My mind screams in protest as I refuse to voice the thoughts and make this harder for both of us.

I put the car into gear and I start to reverse out of the drive. I leave behind my heart and my soul as I wave dejectedly at my husband. I watch him out of the rear-view mirror. I watch until he is a dot in the distance before I start to scream. I scream as I drive and I swear and scream some more. I am so angry and so hurt that I have to leave him. It is so unfair. I feel like a petulant child having a tantrum over something petty, except this isn't petty. My heart is breaking and I can't quite comprehend it all. I will never see him again. I will never see the love of my life again. His soft eyes won't warm me with their mischief. I won't spot someone doing something strange when we are people-watching and find that when I look over to him, he is already staring at me for my reaction. I won't ever have him tell pun after pun until I am covering his mouth with my hand begging him to stop, only for him to lick me. I won't ever have him again. This can't be happening.

I drive continuously, on autopilot, and I couldn't begin to tell you how long I drove for. I know the drive like the back of my hand, having driven to my parents so many times. For Christmas and Thanksgiving. For peace and quiet when Luke and I argue. For celebrations and commiserations. For good and bad, I know this drive like the back of my hand and suddenly I can't drive any further. I slam on the brakes, swerving off into a lay-by; cars sound their horns furiously as they drive past me, angered by my erratic behaviour and driving, but what do they expect? Erratic should be the norm right now. Maybe they haven't heard the news. Maybe they don't know that the world is ending.

I fall out the door and I retch on the side of the road. The heat, despite it being the middle of the night now, sears at my skin and I feel like I am on a Caribbean beach. If only. I let myself be engulfed by my emotions as I bring nothing but bile up. Before long, I am back in the car, doors locked, and I decide to sleep now so I can drive through the early hours of the morning. I set an alarm for three hours' time, only permitting myself that much. I can sleep when I'm dead but I don't want to die in a car crash on the way. I pull on Luke's top, letting his scent engulf my senses and I surround myself in a blanket from the back seat and I try to sleep. I think of all the times Cassie, Luke and I have sat on this blanket on long walks with a picnic. The tears come thick and fast and, before soon, Cassie has nuzzled her way into my lap and is looking up at me, confused by the sounds I'm making. She licks at my hand as if trying to soothe me; if only she knew how grateful I am to still have her with me. I cry until my throat is raw, my eyes are swollen; I feel an almost childlike exhaustion and I slip into a restless sleep, dozing in and out. Dreaming of nothing and everything. I dream of the fire meeting the ground and burning us up and I dream of our ashes that will remain. I wake with a start, crying out in shock as my alarm blares at me and Cassie is barking at me telling me to get up and go. I rub my eyes that have dried up and crusted. I reach for one of the bottles of water in the back to wash my face with and when I look at myself in the mirror, I see nothing but a haunted face of misery. I barely recognise myself. *Time to go, stranger.*

* * *

"Maya?" Luke's voice is a whisper. Despite it being so early, I can't imagine he has wasted any time with his mum by sleeping. "Are you okay?"

"Luke, I'm sorry to call so early but I just wanted to let you know I'm almost there," I whisper, unsure why; I am disturbing no one but everything feels so delicate and fragile that the slightest sound will shatter everything we know.

"I'm glad you're safe," Luke murmurs and I hear him talk to someone in the background. "Go back to sleep, Mum, it's just Maya," he instructs his mum gently and lovingly. *Just Maya.* The is a sting deep in my throat that tries to shred at my confidence in our love.

"Is she still lucid?" I ask, swallowing what feels like razor blades.

"Yes, it's a miracle, I guess. A cruel miracle," he mutters, and I can hear the sulking in his voice.

"I guess I just called to say I love you."

"I love you too," Luke replies and we lapse into silence. A silence that is akin to a first date. Awkward and unknowing. Who says what first? What is too much? More importantly, what is too little?

"Goodbye," I repeat for what feels like the hundredth time.

"Goodbye, Maya." His voice is cold and sad and it's the worst goodbye we could have ever wished for. The phone clicks off as he ends the call and I struggle to soothe my breaths. I am about fifteen minutes away from home, but I wanted to stop to take a last breather and hear his voice for the last time before the end. The calm before the storm. If anything, it has made me feel worse. The longer I drove the hotter it was getting. The air conditioning has

31

never been great in our car and right now, what with the temperature intensifying and I was sweating my ass off.

After finally returning to the road, I drive in a way only one can when they are in their hometown, knowing exactly where I am going. This is home. This is where I grew up. The park is where I had my first kiss with Noah Colman at the age of fifteen. The house on the corner hosted the first house party I went to and where I got so drunk my brothers had to hide me away for the day whilst I recovered. The cinema is where we used to go every Friday night as a family until the boys got too old to be seen with their mum and dad. The high street coffee shops are where I spent endless hours with my best friends chatting about nothing and everything.

I pull into my drive and there they are. My family. Waiting on the doorstep for me, ready for me, my two brothers, red-faced in the heat and sweating, my mum's hair curling and frizzing with the humidity and my dad looking as unaffected as ever. My sweet, perfect family. My brothers run quickly down the steps of the house, and open my door, pulling me out of the car and into their arms. I am engulfed by their love instantly. Despite the searing heat, I bury myself into them, taking in each of their scents and not wanting to let go. Too soon, they pull away.

"Where is Luke?" they all query, my dad ambling down the steps on his walking stick to stand beside my mum.

"He had to stay with his parents," I inform them, trying not to cry once more.

"He left you?" My dad looks taken aback, knowing this is something Luke would never do. His eyes flash with annoyance slightly and I can't help but adore that he still treats me like his little princess, forever needing protecting.

"I couldn't expect him to leave his family whilst I got to spend time with you," I whisper, my heart starting to ache at the thought, a hole there that had been over-spilling with love since the day I met him. "His mum was lucid, properly lucid for the first time in so long," I explain and my mum gasps, tears brimming on her eyelashes.

"Oh love, oh dear," she mutters. "I don't know if that is good or bad," she whispers almost to herself before shaking her head, trying to banish bad thoughts. "Come now, let's all go inside" She waves us all in.

We are suddenly stunned: the heat increases dramatically and we all groan as it hits us, our skin clammy and wet. It makes you feel sluggish to the bone. I look down at Cassie who seems more irritated than usual. She barks at us all, once again annoyed that no one has fussed over her yet and I laugh humourlessly, picking her up and handing her to my mum who immediately gives her the welcome she so desperately wants. Cassie looks at me smugly from my mother's arms and I can't help but be glad someone is happy.

I hook my arms through my brothers, standing between them as they tower over me and lead them indoors. My dad grabs my holdall and Cassie's bed from the car and we all rush inside.

"Can I have a shower, Mum?" I ask and she cocks her eyebrow.

"Only *you* would want to be clean when we are about to die." She lets out a soft and sad laugh and nods. "Be quick."

I nod and I run upstairs, pulling out new clothes. I stink from being in the hot and sweaty car and when the cool water hits me, I feel revived. *Not for much longer.* My subconscious goads me and I ignore it. *It's not the time for you to win*, I berate her for being so cruel. Once refreshed and clean with a new outfit, a soft and flowing white dress to keep me cool, I walk downstairs, holding onto Luke's top that I had taken off when I had woken up, and our wedding album. I think I knew, even then, I wouldn't be arriving here with Luke by my side. I guess I just didn't want to acknowledge it.

"It is getting hotter," Dexter states the obvious and Peter ribs him for it. It feels like normal. They are all sat at the dining room table. My dad at the head of the table and Mum to his right with my empty seat opposite her and Dexter next to me, leaving Peter next to Mum. I settle Cassie's bed down beneath my chair and I grab Cassie along with her comfort toy and lay her in my lap as I sit down next to Dexter. He leans over to stroke Cassie who is adoring the attention, finally not sulking. I hand her one of her treats and she nibbles on it in my lap. My sweet little girl. I look at Dexter and I smile, taking in his soft features. A stark comparison to Peter's strong jawline. They are the complete polar opposites and we often joke that Dexter is the postman's child. It annoys Mom, but Dad only smiles more fondly at his son, for it is Dexter's nature that he got entirely from Dad that proves he is his. As I look around at my family, it strikes me how lucky I am to be with them. So many families will have been torn apart today. What was once a few hours' flight away from each other as a visit is now an impossible task. There will be no reunions for some people, and for many they will simply be alone.

"Love you, little sis." His smile is genuine and there are no longer any signs of torment or teasing, and I hate it.

"I love you too, Dex, and you, Peter." I utter the words, looking to them both. My big brothers. They are supposed to protect me from the world but nothing can protect us now.

"Remember when...?" My mum goes down memory lane and she sips at the wine she has poured myself and her. We chuckle and laugh as the boys snort beer out of their noses as they recount the many pranks they put into action when they were little. Dad sits listening to it all, silent but focused. Sipping slowly on his whiskey. My dad looks at each of us in turn, studying myself, his sons, and his wife. When he looks at me, I look back and he gives me a soft smile. He reaches out his hand to me and I take it. I use my other hand to open up my wedding album and look at the front picture: Luke and I embracing, having just said "I do." I think about our wedding and how the thunderstorm that hit that day almost wiped out the large tent that was hosting our wedding. So many points when we had to reconsider getting married that day, cancelling and postponing, but without even seeing one another, we had both told the person in charge of the event, one way or another, we were getting married. Even if we had to stand in the pouring rain. The clouds had finally broken half an hour before I was intending to walk down the aisle and the sun had shone down on us as we said, 'I do.' It's ironic that we wanted nothing more than for the sun to help bring our wedding to a success; now it's tearing us apart. I look at the picture for as long as I can, as we continue to recall countless memories. I can barely swallow as I try to gulp back the tears that are coming. My mum is already in floods but she keeps going. She has remembered everything. Such a stark contrast to Rose. Dexter grabs my hand as well as Peter's, and as Mum, Dad and Peter join up, we complete the circle. We can feel the heat and we don't talk about it. We just talk endlessly.

I can't tell you when it ended. I can't tell you if it hurt. It feels like we just kept sitting there talking for eternity. We are together and even though I am without my soulmate, I know this was the only way. The best way. I think of him continually and by doing so with my family here together, I will continue to think of him and reminisce with my family forever.

The world came to an end that day. The heat overcame us and turned us to ashes. We were enveloped by the sun's scorching arms. We were engulfed.